Caillou

The Magic of Compost

Adaptation of the animated series: Sarah Margaret Johanson
Illustrations: CINAR Animation; adapted by Eric Sévigny

Caillou loved spending the day
with his grandma.
"Grandma, look! I'm a magician!
Abracadabra!" Caillou said.
He really wanted to be a magician
and do amazing magic tricks.
"Do you think you can make a
lunch disappear?" Grandma
asked.
"Oh, yes!" Caillou answered.

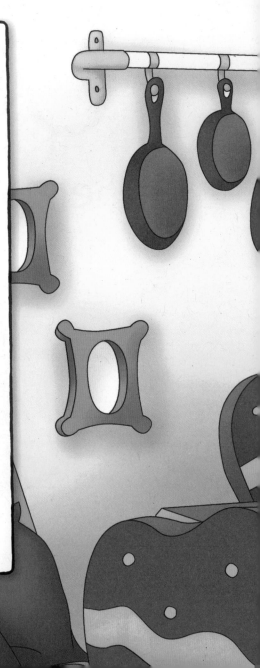

After lunch, Grandma dropped the banana peel into a small bucket beside the door. Caillou was curious, so he looked in the bucket.
"Is that your garbage can?" Caillou asked.
"No, it's not," Grandma replied.
Caillou made a face. "But it's all gooshy and yucky."
"I need it for my garden," Grandma explained.
"Your garden?" Caillou asked.
"Come, I'll show you."

Grandma took the bucket outside and went to a large barrel. She took the lid off and dumped the contents of the bucket inside.

"Is that a garbage can?" Caillou asked.

"No, it's a composter," Grandma explained. "I put in food scraps like fruit and vegetables, but no meat and no dairy. That means no cheese or milk."

"I put all the leaves, grass clippings, and weeds in here too, and add a little water," Grandma explained.

"It must be *really* yucky in there!" Caillou said.

"Ah, but that's the surprising thing. Inside this composter all the messy, yucky stuff turns into something completely different," Grandma explained.

"Like a magic trick?" Caillou asked, amazed.

"Yes, it is rather like a magic trick. Would you like to see what it turns into?" Grandma asked.

"Yes, please!"

Grandma pulled up a small panel at the bottom. Caillou leaned in closer to see black dirt spilling out!

"It's dirt! Did all that stuff turn into dirt?" Caillou asked.

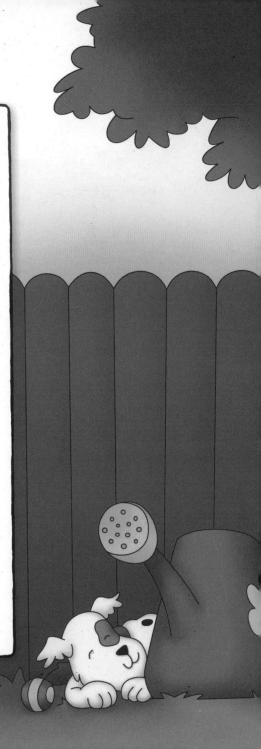

"It's not dirt. It's called compost, and it takes weeks and weeks to happen."

"A composter makes compost," Caillou said.

Grandma shoveled some compost into a wheelbarrow and took it to a flowerbed. "That's right. Compost is nice, rich soil that helps my plants to grow," Grandma explained.

"Wow, that's the best magic trick ever!" Caillou was impressed.

As soon as he got home, Caillou went to the kitchen cupboards and pulled out a plastic container. After supper, he put the dinner scraps into his container. Potato skins, bread crusts, and corn, but no cheese – that's dairy.

"Caillou, what are you up to?" Mommy asked.

"I'm going to show you the best magic trick ever," he said. "I'm going to change all of this yucky stuff into plant food, but we need to get a composter."

Daddy got a nice large composter.
Every time Daddy cut the grass,
he put the clippings into the
composter. Caillou put Mommy's
teabags and his apple cores
into the composter. Every day
something was added to the
composter.
Caillou looked inside week after
week, but everything looked the
same. He started to think his magic
trick wasn't working.

Caillou waited a whole month.
It seemed like days and days,
but the wait was finally over.
"Come on, everybody!" Caillou
called.
He was excited to show everyone
his big magic trick. He reached
the composter and waited while
everyone gathered around.
Caillou was a little worried. What
if it didn't work?

Caillou got his courage up and put on his show.

"It's time for the best magic trick ever: turning food and grass and leaves and water into compost. That's plant food," Caillou said.

He turned to the composter and waved his hands.

"Abracadabra, COMPOST!"

Caillou kneeled and put his hands on the bottom panel.

Everyone leaned in close. Caillou pulled the panel aside and a small amount of black compost spilled out. Caillou grinned from ear to ear.

"Ta-daaaa!" Caillou yelled.

"How wonderful!" Mommy applauded.

"Hooray!" Daddy cheered.

"For my next trick, I'm going to use my new compost to grow flowers," Caillou said.

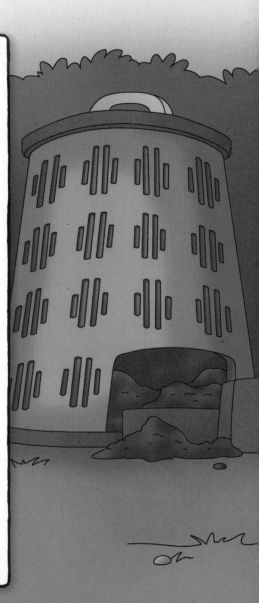

CAILLOU is a registered trademark of Chouette Publishing (1987) Inc.

Text adapted by Sarah Margaret Johanson from the scenario of the CAILLOU animated
film series produced by Cookie Jar Entertainment Inc. (© 1997 Caillou Productions (2004) Inc.,
a subsidiary of Cookie Jar Entertainment Inc.).
All rights reserved.
Original scenario written by Kim Thompson.
Original episode no 514: Caillou can compost.
Illustrations taken from the television series CAILLOU and adapted by Eric Sévigny.
Art Direction: Monique Dupras

The PBS KIDS logo is a registered mark of PBS and is used with permission.

We acknowledge the financial support of the Government of Canada through
the Canada Book Fund for our publishing activities.

Canadian   Patrimoine
Heritage   canadien

We acknowledge the support of the Ministry of Culture and Communications
of Quebec and SODEC for the publication and promotion of this book.

SODEC
Québec

Bibliothèque et Archives nationales du Québec and Library
and Archives Canada cataloguing in publication

Johanson, Sarah Margaret, 1968-
Caillou: the magic of compost
(Ecology club)
For children aged 3 and up.

ISBN 978-2-89450-773-5

1. Green manuring - Juvenile literature. I. Sévigny, Eric. II. Title. III. Title: Magic of compost.

S661.J63 2011   j631.8'75 C2010-941997-9

Legal deposit: 2011

Recycled
Supporting responsible use
of forest resources
www.fsc.org Cert no. SGS-COC-004340
© 1996 Forest Stewardship Council

The use of entirely recycled paper
produced locally, containing
chlorine-free 100% post-consumer
content, saved 69 mature trees.

Printed in Canada
10 9 8 7 6 5 4 3 2 1